Mystery of Broken Wheel Ranch

Mystery of

Coordinating Editor
MORTON BOTEL, ED.D.
Assistant Superintendent and Reading Consultant,
Bucks County Public Schools, Doylestown, Pennsylvania.

Elementary Advisor
CORA L. HOLSCLAW, M.S.
Assistant Superintendent in charge of Elementary Education,
Pennsbury Schools, Fallsington, Pennsylvania.

Secondary Advisor
GLORIA C. CAMMAROTA, ED.D.
Assistant Superintendent and Curriculum Consultant,
Bucks County Public Schools, Doylestown, Pennsylvania.

Broken Wheel Ranch

by Leonard Eisner

Juv
E36
My

Illustrated by Wm. Francis Taylor

Follett Publishing Company   *Chicago*

Copyright © 1961 by
Follett Publishing Company
Chicago
All rights reserved.
No portion of this book may be
reproduced in any form without
express permission of the publisher.
Printed in U.S.A.

Library of Congress Catalog Card Number: 61-16923

CAN YOU READ THIS BOOK?*

Every word in this book has been carefully checked to make sure you understand the stories completely. Before you begin *Mystery of Broken Wheel Ranch,* take the test below.

Read the words in the list to someone. Keep a score of the words you get right. Then check the Reading Box Score to see how well you can read this book.

1. ago	11. leg
2. believe	12. move
3. butter	13. pick
4. count	14. queer
5. drive	15. rope
6. fall	16. shout
7. flower	17. spot
8. great	18. suit
9. hold	19. trip
10. kind	20. while

READING BOX SCORE

YOUR SCORE	
10-13	This book is probably too hard for you.
14-16	You can probably read this book with help on some words.
17-18	This book is probably easy for you.
19-20	This book is probably very easy for you.

*See Teacher's Manual of the *Interesting Reading Series*

CONCORDIA COLLEGE LIBRARY
BRONXVILLE. N. Y. 10708

CHAPTER I

Red, the ranch foreman, pulled the truck up to the house. Bob and Ted were tired from the long train ride but they jumped out and ran for the porch. As they climbed the front steps a cowboy came out of the door.

"Hi, Lefty," Red said. "What's up?"

"Will's hurt. His horse stepped in a hole and threw him."

"Where is he? Did you get the doctor?"

"He's up in his bed," said Lefty. "The doc says his leg's broken."

Red and the boys ran into the house and up the stairs. The doctor was just coming out of the bedroom.

"How is he, Doc?" asked Red. "Will he be all right?"

"I've set his leg. He'll be fine in six weeks or so."

Bob and Ted went into the room. "Hi, Uncle Will. Sorry about your leg."

"Hello, there, boys. It's good to see you! Don't be sorry about my leg. I need a rest anyway. Doc says I'll be as good as new in six weeks." He smiled but the boys could see he was in pain.

"This is just great," said Red. "It would have to happen right at roundup time. We were short of hands, but this . . ."

"You'll have to take over for me, Red. You know how much this roundup means. I know you won't let me down."

Red looked down at the man on the bed. "I'll do my best."

"Can we help?" asked Bob.

"You sure can!" Uncle Will said. "If you two help out around here, it will free all the hands for the roundup."

"Can you boys ride?" Red wanted to know.

"Sure they can ride. They've been riding ever since they

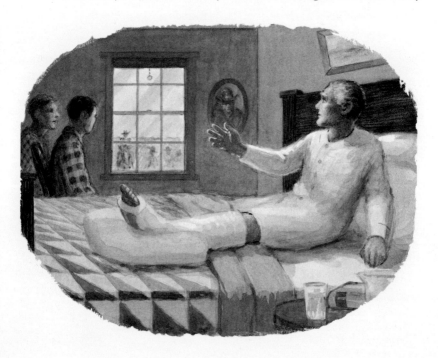

were old enough to get on a horse. After a few days no one will know they're from a farm back East."

"O. K., Will. I'll get the roundup started. I'll see you fellows later." Red left and the boys heard him calling the cowboys.

"Welcome to the Broken Wheel Ranch," said Uncle Will. "I'm sorry I couldn't get down to meet your train. I was too busy breaking my leg."

"We're glad to be here! We've been waiting for spring vacation so we could come out. That's all we've thought about ever since you bought this ranch. Now we're going to be real cowboys!" Ted had a big smile on his face.

"It will be a big help to have you here. I'm counting on you to help Red all you can. We'll be in a bad way if we don't have a good roundup."

"What do you mean?" asked Bob.

"The ranch always made money. But in the last two or three years no one has looked after it. I had to borrow money to buy the ranch and some more to put it in shape. If I don't have a good roundup, I could lose it."

"Gee! I didn't think it was like that," said Ted.

"I haven't told any of the hands. I brought Red here with me. He knows all about it. The rest of the men were hired in town. We don't want them to start looking for new jobs. You can see why this has to be a good roundup."

"We sure can," said Bob. "And we'll help! What are we

9

waiting for? Why don't we start working now?"

"O. K., boys. Now you do what Red tells you. He's running things until I get out of this bed. We'll have to get you some working clothes. Tell Red I said you need boots and hats."

The boys left their uncle in his room and went to find Red. They told him about the boots and hats.

"I have to go back to town for some other things," he said. "Hop in the truck and we'll fix you up, too."

Soon the boys were in a store where all kinds of clothes for cowboys were sold. There were fancy shirts and light-colored pants, too.

"I'd sure feel silly in those things," said Red. "I wouldn't be able to do any work. I'd be afraid of getting dirty."

The boys went with Red to the hat counter. They looked until they found some hats that were like Red's.

"I'd like one like that."

"So would I." The hats the boys wanted were black and had strings to hold them on while they were riding.

Then the boys looked at boots. They each picked up a pair like Red's.

"That's the idea," said Red. "You need these to work in. You don't have to look pretty."

"Why do cowboy boots have high heels?" Bob was wondering how he would walk in them.

"They keep your feet from going too far into the stirrups," said Red. "The pointed toes make it easy to get your feet into the stirrups in a hurry."

The boys put on their new hats and boots in the store. When they left, they felt like real cowboys. They even looked like real cowboys, but they didn't walk like cowboys. They walked as if their feet hurt.

"You'll get used to the boots," Red laughed. "It'll take a little time, that's all. Now let's get on back home."

As they rode, Bob asked Red, "What's that thing painted on the side of the truck?"

"That's your uncle's brand, the Broken Wheel."

"I remember now," said Ted. "When Uncle Will wrote

to us last fall about the ranch, he said it was named the Broken Wheel. How did it get that name, Red?"

"Well," said Red, "the man who built the ranch came to this part of the country a long time ago. He had to drive his wagon across Rock River, a few miles there to the east. As he came out of the water, the wagon hit a rock and broke a wheel. He looked around and saw good grass land. There was plenty of water from the river. I guess he figured this would be a good place for a ranch. So he started a herd and build a house up on the hill. When he picked his brand, he remembered why he had stopped where he did. He called his ranch the Broken Wheel.

12

The old wheel is hanging in the hall in the old part of the house."

When they got back to the ranch, Red took the boys to their room. "You get cleaned up. We'll eat in a little while. Tomorrow we'll get you some horses and find out what kind of cowboys you are."

CHAPTER II

In the morning, the boys were up with the sun. They could hardly wait to see their horses.

"All right," said Red, "let's go out to the corral. We've got horses all picked out for you."

In the corral were two horses a little smaller than the rest.

Bob pointed to them. "Are they the ones, Red?"

"Yes they are, boys. How do you like them?"

"They're beautiful!" said Ted. "What are their names?"

"We call the brown one Dusty and the black-and-white one Storm. Take your pick."

The boys walked up to the corral fence to get a better look.

The horses walked up to the fence to look at the boys. Storm went to Ted, and Dusty went to Bob.

"It looks as if the horses picked you out, boys."

"That's all right. We really couldn't decide anyway."

"Saddle up," said Red, "and let's go out to where the men are working."

Bob and Ted saddled their horses and mounted. "Let's go!"

As they rode, Red told Bob and Ted about ranching.

"We let the cattle run free all winter. They get plenty to eat and lots of good water. In the spring we round them up and put our brand on the new calves."

Red showed the boys how the cowboys were heating the branding iron. They watched while one man roped a young steer and another man branded him.

"Doesn't that hurt?" Bob made a face.

"It hurts him only a little, but it scares him a lot."

"Why do you have to brand them?" asked Bob.

"If our steers get into someone else's herd, we can get them back."

Back at the house a little later, the boys had lunch with their uncle. Then Red showed them how to use a rope. He left them to work at it. They tried again and again to drop their ropes around a rock. First they tried it on foot. After many tries, Ted began to rope the rock once in a while. Soon after, Bob was beginning to get it, too.

"Now we'll have to learn to do it on horseback, Ted. We can't chase cattle on foot."

Just then Red came out of the house. He smiled as he watched the boys work. "Keep it up, boys. Soon you'll be better than any of the cowboys."

The boys smiled and kept trying. Bob rode up to the rock on one side, and Ted rode up on the other. Both boys threw

16

their ropes at the same time. Red shouted, as both ropes caught the rock, "Good work! Now you've earned a rest. We'll take a ride and I'll show you some more of the ranch."

Red got his horse and rode off with Bob and Ted. They rode for a long while.

"What's that over there?" Ted pointed to a big white square lying on the ground.

"That's a salt lick. Haven't you seen other pieces around? The cattle like it. Sometimes you can find salt right in the ground. I haven't seen it on the Broken Wheel yet. The cattle stay where they have water to drink, grass to eat, and salt to lick."

"I'd hate to get lost out here," Bob said, looking at the flat land all around.

"It's very hard to get lost on the Broken Wheel, boys. Do you see that hill over there?" Red pointed to a big hill. The

rocky sides went almost straight up. "Well, you can see that hill from almost any place on the ranch. If you climb to the top of the hill, you can see the house. No one gets lost here.

"Why don't you ride up near there and take a look around?" he went on. "We'll start you working tomorrow. Listen for the big bell. When it rings slowly, it says, 'Time to eat.' If it sounds like a fire truck, come a-running because something's wrong." Red left them and rode back to the corral.

"Come on, Bob. I'll race you to the fence over there."

The boys galloped off. Bob got Dusty off to a fast start. Ted

quickly caught up and slowly moved in front. Storm got to the fence just ahead of Dusty.

"Let's ride along the fence. We can see how far around we can get before we have to turn back for dinner."

The boys rode for a long time. When they came to the river, they stopped to let the horses drink. "This must be Rock River," said Bob. "I wonder which rock the wagon hit."

"We'll have to ask Uncle Will. Do you think his land ends here? Look at that brook. It looks as if it comes out of that rocky hill over there."

"Say, Ted, we ought to start heading back. It's getting late and we're a long way from the ranch house."

The boys rode back toward the big hill Red had showed them. The horses had to go slowly because of the big rocks on the path. Just then the ranch bell went clang-clang-clang-clang-clang . . .

"That's not the dinner bell. Something's wrong! Let's ride, Bob."

The boys raced back to the house. Cowboys were riding up from all over. Red was waiting in front of the house.

"What's wrong?" asked Ted.

"Yeah, Red, what's up?" asked Lefty.

"All the steers we branded yesterday are gone! Will told me to take over until his leg gets better. I'm doing great! As soon as I start running the roundup, we lose over a hundred head."

"Gone!" "How can they be gone!" "What happened to them!" The cowboys couldn't believe what they had heard.

"What do we do, Red?" asked Lefty.

"Let's get moving. We have a little while before it gets dark. Maybe we can find those steers."

The cowboys rode off. Bob and Ted were tired, and so were the horses. But they wanted to help.

"Why don't we ride back and climb up the big hill, Ted? Maybe we can see something from there."

Dusty and Storm walked slowly up the big hill. They

20

The Broken Wheel Brand

stepped carefully over the rocks. When they were at the top, the boys looked all around.

"There's no place on the ranch those steers could hide!"

It began to get dark so the boys turned the horses to go back.

"Look, Bob! What's that fire over there?"

"It looks like a camp fire. That's on the other side of the fence, isn't it?"

"Come on, Bob. Let's see what we can find out down there."

The boys didn't feel tired anymore. They raced toward the little fire. From the fence they could see a man cooking. Behind him was a tent.

21

"Hey, Ted. I wonder what he's doing here?"

The boys heard something. "Sounds like steers, Bob."

One of the steers came into the light of the campfire.

"Look at the brand, Ted. Doesn't it look like the Broken Wheel?"

"I wish we had more light. I can't really tell."

CHAPTER III

Bob and Ted rode back to the ranch house. They saw Lefty when they rode up.

"Where's Red?" asked Bob.

"He's not back yet. You'd better walk your horses, fellows, so they'll cool off. If you don't, they'll get sick."

The boys took off the saddles and walked Dusty and Storm. When the horses were cooled off, the boys rubbed them down and put them in the corral.

After the horses were fed, Bob and Ted walked to the house. They were sitting on the steps when Red rode up.

"Did you see anything, boys?"

"We saw some cattle," said Bob. But we're not sure they're Broken Wheel steers."

"Where was this?"

"We were at the top of the big hill," said Ted. "We saw a little fire, so we went over to have a look."

"What did you find?"

"A tall man with black hair was cooking over the fire. He had a tent and some cattle."

"Oh, that was probably that new man, Chuck Millar. Bought some land next to the Broken Wheel a month ago. But he never had cattle before. How many does he have?"

"We couldn't tell. They made a lot of noise, though," said Bob.

"It was pretty dark," said Ted; "but we did see one steer, Red. The brand did look something like the Broken Wheel."

"We don't know much about Millar but it doesn't seem possible that he took the cattle. He never says much to anybody. But I'm sure he's honest. You take a ride out there tomorrow. I'm sure you'll find the steers aren't ours."

"Are you going to tell Uncle Will about the missing steers?" asked Bob.

"No. The doctor gave him something to make him sleep, so he didn't hear the bell. He doesn't know anything about them yet. I don't know how to tell him."

"Well," said Ted, "the steers may not be lost. You'd only make him feel bad for nothing."

24

"If we don't turn up those steers tomorrow, I'll have to tell him," said Red. "Don't say anything about Millar to anyone. There may be nothing to it—and we don't want to start any false stories."

"We'll take a ride out there tomorrow anyway. Maybe we can find out something about him."

"O. K.," said Red. "But don't let him know you're looking for missing steers."

CHAPTER IV

Right after breakfast the next day, the cook made up a lunch and the boys took off. They rode until they could see the tent. Millar was near by, working.

"I wonder what he's building, Ted."

"Let's watch and see. Maybe we can find out."

As they rode slowly along the fence they watched Millar dig small holes and drive poles into them. Then he tied ropes around the poles to make a fence.

"That looks like a corral," said Bob. "Let's tell Red."

"No, we'll wait and see what else he does, Bob."

"Why don't we go up and talk to him?"

"I don't know if that's a good idea," said Ted. "Ranch people are supposed to be friendly, but this Millar doesn't seem to be friendly at all."

"Come on, Ted. He won't hurt us."

The boys tied their horses to the fence and climbed over. They walked up to the tent.

The boys didn't know what to say. They stood quietly, watching. After a while, Ted started, "Hello. I'm Ted and this is Bob. We're working for the Broken Wheel."

Mr. Millar stopped what he was doing. He looked at the boys for a few moments. There was no smile on his face. Finally he said, "I am Charles Millar. This is my land." Then he turned back to his work.

The boys could tell the conversation was over. They walked back to the fence.

"I wonder why he's angry," said Bob.

"I don't think he was angry, Bob. Maybe he doesn't like strangers on his land."

"Did Red say Millar had bought the land?" asked Bob.

"Sure. He wouldn't build that big corral on someone else's land."

The boys stayed at the fence and watched Millar work. Now he was building a gate for his corral.

"I wonder what he's going to put in the corral, Bob. He

doesn't have any horses except for the one tied to the tent."

"Maybe he's going to use it to brand cattle in."

"But the steer we saw last night already had a brand," said Ted.

"Yeah, but it may have been Uncle Will's brand."

"Then he'd have to change the brand, wouldn't he?"

"We can come back here later and see what he puts into the corral," said Bob.

"All right. Let's ride around the ranch some more. Maybe we can find Uncle Will's cattle."

The boys rode for the rest of the morning. They stopped to climb a hill. From the top they could see Uncle Will's cowboys rounding up the great herd. An ocean of black cattle was moving toward the big corral.

When the boys got hungry, they sat down under a big tree to eat their lunch. They talked about the missing cattle.

"Let's ride back to see what Millar is doing now, Ted." Once again, the boys rode across the fields and up to the fence. They tied the horses to the fence and sat down to watch the tall man work.

The corral was finished, and Millar had started to work on what looked like the beginning of a house. He worked without looking up.

"I'm sure he sees us, Ted." Bob spoke in a quiet voice. "I guess he doesn't want to talk to us."

"He's trying to move that big log. Let's see if we can help him."

"Why should we do that?" asked Bob. "He's not very friendly."

"Maybe that's because he doesn't know us, Bob. If we help him, he may talk more. Maybe we can find out some more

about that brand we saw."

Bob followed Ted up to the new corral.

"Can we help you, Mr. Millar?"

The man looked up, but didn't say anything. Then he started to work again.

30

"That's a big log," said Bob. "Will you let us help you?"

Millar looked up again. "You boys sound like you're from the East?" His voice was deep and clear. The boys were surprised at the way he talked. He didn't sound like any of the cowboys. Millar went on. "I'm from the East, too, from a big city. I came out here to be away from all the people. I will do my work alone." He started to work again.

Bob and Ted knew there was no more to say. They went back to their horses, looking around as they walked.

"Do you think he's afraid we'll find something?" asked Ted.

"I don't know. Maybe he just doesn't want any outsiders around."

"We'll have to look around some more. I just don't know about this fellow. Red says he's O. K. But why won't he talk to us?"

"Did you see all the cattle out behind the trees?"

"Must have been over a hundred."

"Yes, but I hope you could make out the brand better than I."

"I could just about make it out. It looked a little like the Broken Wheel, but it may be something else."

"We'll have to get closer to those steers next time," said Bob. "If Millar's brand is too much like Uncle Will's, he may be taking Broken Wheel steers and fixing up the brands."

"Right, Bob. And if the steers are Millar's, we may be able to find out where he gets them."

CHAPTER V

The boys found Red at the Broken Wheel corral.

"Millar's got some young steers," said Ted, "about a hundred, I'd say."

"Did you see the brand?"

"We couldn't get near enough to see it well," said Bob. "It does look something like the Broken Wheel."

"I still don't believe it. I'm sure Millar is as honest as anyone around here. Anyway, I can't do anything until I know more about the brand. You fellows, better not say anything about all this. Keep looking in on him if you want. I'm sure he didn't get his herd on this side of the fence. But if he did . . ."

"We'll find out about it if he did," said Bob.

"I'll get Lefty to show you how to fix fences. Then you can keep busy and ride around at the same time. No one will think you're just looking around."

"Good idea, Red. We saw some breaks in the fence that we can take care of."

That afternoon, Lefty showed Bob and Ted how to tell if a fence was strong. When they found a broken wire or a loose post, he showed them how to fix it. They rode until they found a break. Lefty watched while the boys worked.

Then he gave the boys a roll of wire. "I think you know how to take care of a broken fence."

"We'll do the best we can."

The boys rode off along the fence. They saw small breaks, but none big enough to drive a hundred steers through. After awhile, they rode to the top of the big hill.

"Look," said Bob. "We can see Millar's whole ranch from here."

"I can see his herd, but I don't see him anywhere."

"Maybe he's going to be away for a while. I'd really like to see that brand of his close up."

Just then they saw Millar riding up. He was driving another herd of young steers.

"Look at that!" said Ted. Then, he looked around at the Broken Wheel ranch house. Someone was riding hard toward the house.

"That looks like Lefty's horse. He must have big news," said Bob.

"Let's go, Bob. We'll see what's up."

When Bob and Ted rode up Lefty and Red were talking to some of the other cowboys.

Red called to the boys. "Glad you're here, fellows. What did you find out about Millar?"

"All we know," said Ted, "is that he's building a ranch

and he has a herd of young steers. We can't get close enough to see the brand too well, but from far away it looks something like the Broken Wheel."

"Anything else, Bob?"

"Only that he doesn't like people looking around."

"One more thing," said Ted. "We saw him just now, and he was driving some new steers. He must have nearly two hundred by now."

"Do we need to hear anymore?" asked Lefty. "We lose steers and Millar gets new ones. That's good enough for me. Let's go get our animals."

"Hold on!" said Red. "We don't do anything until we can prove he has our cattle.

"We lost another hundred last night. But we've found a few of the ones we had lost before. I can't figure this at all."

"Gee, if Millar or anyone else had taken them, he wouldn't be sending any back, would he?" Bob couldn't understand it either.

"Does Uncle Will know?" asked Ted.

"I was just going to tell him. You fellows come on up with me."

Red walked slowly up to Will's bedroom. The boys followed him. They hoped that their uncle wouldn't be too hard on Red.

Red told the story of the missing cattle. Will listened quietly until he was done. The boys thought he was going to blow up. But he didn't. "Red," he said, "you're my friend. We've worked together a long time. I know you're doing your best. But don't forget, if we don't get our cattle back, we're all washed up. I won't be able to pay the bank. You won't have a job, and I won't have a ranch."

Red smiled a little. "I'm glad you still believe in me."

"Now, enough of this," said Will. "What are we going to do about those steers, Red?"

"All we can do is look. I don't think they're on the ranch anywhere, but they may be."

"Millar can't have them! He wouldn't take them and keep them on land right next to ours."

"I don't think he took the cattle," said Red. "It would be foolish. He's keeping them just outside your fence. We've never seen his brand up close, but we know it's something like the Broken Wheel brand."

"I wish we could find something to prove it one way or another," said Bob.

"Tell you what," said Will. "You boys ride over there again tomorrow and try to get close to those steers. Keep talking to Millar. Maybe he'll let something out. Just watch yourselves."

"We've tried, Uncle Will, but we'll try it again."

"Red," said Will, "you take the truck into town right now. Stay as long as you have to. Talk to everyone who buys and sells cattle. See if anyone has been selling cattle with our brand. And try to find out where Millar has been buying his cattle."

36

"What will that prove?" asked Bob.

"If he buys the steers, he didn't take them from us."

"But what if he didn't buy them?"

"Then we still have to prove he took them," said Will. "Now get going."

"Anything you want while I'm in town?" asked Red.

"Yeah. Two hundred head of my cattle."

CHAPTER VI

The boys had forgotten about dinner. Walking downstairs, they suddenly felt hungry. They went into the kitchen.

"Sorry, boys," said Buzz, the cook, "there's no more pie."

"Oh, come on, Buzz. We want pie and everything else you've got. It's been a long day!"

"That's fine!" said Buzz. "You come in just when the dishes are all washed."

"We'll do ours when we finish," said Bob, "but stay and talk to us while we eat."

38

Buzz put out some food for the boys. "What do you want to talk about?"

"The missing cattle," said Ted. "What do you think happened to them?"

"I really couldn't say, fellows. Sometimes steers just get lost."

"Do you think Millar took them?"

"I don't think so," said Buzz. "Out here, some people don't think much of strangers, but that's not fair. This Millar seems O. K. to me."

"You know," said Ted, "I'm sorry we ever saw that campfire. I wish now we could be sure once and for all that Millar didn't take the cattle."

"The best way to do that is for you to find the missing steers," said Buzz.

"We know, but we don't know where to look."

"If you knew where to look, it wouldn't be any fun," Buzz went on. "You have to think like a steer. Ask yourself, 'Where would I go if I were a steer?'

"My guess is that the cattle just walked away," said Buzz. "If you can guess why they walked, you'll probably find them."

"We'll have to keep our eyes wide open tomorrow when we talk to Millar," said Bob. "If he is taking the cattle, I'll be mad at him."

"If you boys are going to keep your eyes open tomorrow, you'd better finish up and get some sleep."

39

As the boys were going up to bed, some of the men rode up. They ran into the house and said, "More young steers are lost. We can't find the ones we branded today."

"What are you going to do?" asked Bob. "Are you going after Millar?"

"No," said Lefty. "We'll wait until tomorrow. We have to talk with Red first. But if Millar has a bunch of new cattle, he'd better have a good story."

CHAPTER VII

The next morning the boys were early for breakfast. They asked Uncle Will what the men had found the night before.

"The cowboys rode all the way around the fence, but they didn't find anything," he said.

"Did Red get back from town?"

"Yes, but he couldn't find out very much. Nobody has bought any cattle. Nobody has sold any cattle."

"What about Mr. Millar, Uncle Will?"

"Everyone in town says he isn't the kind to steal. They say he had a bad time back East. First, his wife died, then, his two sons. Now he just wants to be alone."

"We still don't know where the cattle went," said Bob.

"You boys take a ride out to Millar's place," said Uncle Will. "Don't say anything about our missing cattle. Just look around again."

Bob and Ted got their horses and rode toward Millar's ranch. They saw Millar standing beside his tent.

"Look, Ted, he has new steers. Both times Uncle Will had lost steers the night before."

"That sure doesn't look good for him," said Ted. "But it still doesn't mean that he took Uncle Will's cattle."

The man looked up and saw the boys. "Hello, Mr. Millar," said Ted. "I see you have some more cattle."

"Yes," said Bob. "When did you get them?"

"They came last night." Millar turned to walk away.

"But where did you get them?" asked Bob.

"Get away from here and stop asking questions." Millar was angry.

The boys didn't know what to say. They turned to go to tell Uncle Will that Millar had some more cattle.

As they rode, they met Red and Lefty. "Did you find out anything?" asked Red.

"No," said Bob. "We tried to get him to talk about his cattle, but he didn't want to. He must have about two hundred head now."

"And we lost just about two hundred," said Lefty. "He must have taken them."

"I don't know," Red shook his head. "The same days that Millar has new steers, the Broken Wheel has lost steers. Maybe they *are* Will's cattle."

The four rode back to the ranch house.

When the boys had told their uncle what they had seen, Will said, "We still don't know for sure whether Millar took any of our steers. But we'll find out. Keep a close watch all night. If he is taking them, we can catch him red-handed."

42

"If we lose any cattle tonight, that fellow had better not have any new steers tomorrow." Red's face was hard.

"But if you don't see him take them," said Ted, "you don't know whose steers he has."

"He won't tell you where he got them," said Lefty. "Do you want to wait until he has the whole Broken Wheel herd?"

Ted didn't say anything. He was more confused than ever.

CHAPTER VIII

After lunch the boys rode for a while, but they didn't find any fences broken. They rode up a rocky path that led to the river. Nearby, they found a little brook and good grass for their horses. Then they found a cool spot for themselves and sat down to rest.

After a while, Ted got up. "Let's get the horses. We have a lot more fence to look at today." They walked around to the place where they had left them. Dusty and Storm were gone.

"What's going on around here! We had better stay together, Bob, or first thing you know, one of us will be gone!"

"That's not so funny. It just might happen!" Bob looked worried.

The boys walked all around the rocks, but there was no sign of the horses.

They looked for tracks, but the horses had left none. "I guess they're lost, Ted. I wonder if Millar has two new horses."

"We'd better start walking," said Ted. "It's a long way back to the house."

The boys walked for a long time.

"These boots weren't meant for walking," said Ted. "My feet are killing me. I hope it's not much farther." Finally, the boys got to the house. They sat down on the front steps and pulled off their boots. Buzz came out to see who was there.

"Howdy, boys. Why are you so tired?" The boys told him what had happened to the horses.

"They'll come back," said Buzz. "They like what we feed them better than grass."

"But where could they be?" asked Bob.

Ted thought for a minute. Then he asked, "Buzz, if a horse has cool water and good grass, and he's in the shade, what else could he want?"

"Well, could be he would want salt. Sometimes a horse licks salt just as the steers do."

"But there was no salt up there, only rocks," said Bob. "Do you think the horses are around there? Should we get other horses and ride out after them?"

"No," said Buzz, "they'll be back soon. Wait a while. If they don't show up, then you can go out and look for them."

CHAPTER IX

The boys tried to wait, but they were worried.

"How can we tell Uncle Will we lost the horses? He'll never forgive us."

"Let's get horses and ride out after them."

The boys asked Buzz to help saddle two new horses. Soon they were back at the rocks. There was no sign of Dusty and Storm. The boys called and called, but the horses did not come to them.

"What are we going to do, Ted? We can't just go up to Uncle Will and tell him that we lost those two wonderful horses."

"I think I have an idea. Remember what Buzz told us about the lost cattle? He said that we should try to think as a steer thinks. Maybe the horses did that for us. If Dusty and Storm went after salt, maybe that's where the missing cattle went, too."

"Do you mean that if we find the horses, we'll find the cattle?"

"That's the idea," said Ted. "We'll just let some cattle find the salt for us."

"I don't get it."

"Look," said Ted. "Uncle Will always kept newly branded cattle near here. These steers had been out on the range, and they knew where they would find salt. When they moved here, they couldn't get to the old salt licks. So they must have found new ones. They must have found the same ones that our horses found."

"But that doesn't tell us where to look," said Bob.

"The horses were right here when we lost them, Bob. The salt must be around here somewhere, too."

"But how can we find it?" asked Bob.

"We can't find it, but cattle can. We'll ride out and rope two steers. Then we'll tie them with long ropes at the same spot we tied the horses. Sooner or later they'll want salt, and if it's around here, they'll find it. All we have to do is wait until they're gone and follow the ropes."

"It might work," said Bob, "*if* the missing cattle and our horses *did* get lost looking for salt."

The boys rode back to tell Buzz their plan.

"It just might work. I'll find you some long ropes."

Buzz went to the store room and soon came back with the ropes. Before they left, Ted asked, "Did the men find any sign of the cattle?"

"No," said Buzz, "and they're beginning to think that Millar had something to do with it. They're going to stay out there all night tonight."

"What will happen if Millar has our cattle?" asked Bob.

"There will be a lot of trouble, I think," said Buzz.

"I hope our idea works and we find our cattle."

The boys found two steers out on the range.

"Let's rope them." The boys each rode out after a steer, swinging their ropes the way Red had shown them. After a few tries, the ropes dropped over the steers' heads.

"Hurry, Bob," said Ted. "Let's get them to the rocks and the little brook."

The boys led the steers to the rocks as fast as they could. When they got there, they tied the long ropes around the steers.

"With the steers tied this way, they won't get hurt if the ropes get caught on something."

The boys tied the other ends of the long ropes to trees and rode away.

"We'll have to leave them alone," said Ted. "The steers may not go after the salt if they see us."

When the boys were out of sight of the steers, they stopped and tied up the horses. Then they walked quietly back to a place near where they had tied the steers.

Both steers were standing where the boys had left them. One of them was eating the grass. The boys watched for a long time. The steers hardly moved. They drank water from the little brook that ran out of the wall. They ate a little more grass.

"Let's make them move around," said Bob.

"No! If we do, we might scare them. Then they won't

think about salt." The boys waited.

"What if they don't go after the salt?" asked Bob. "What if there is no salt at all?"

"Then we'll know that our idea is all wrong and we'll have to let someone else find the steers."

The boys waited some more.

"Let's do something, Ted. We can't just stand here."

"Let's ride up to the big hill. Maybe we can see something from there."

The boys got their horses and rode to the hill. Then they tied up the horses and climbed to the top. They could see all around the ranch. They couldn't see Dusty and Storm anywhere. They did see many, many cattle, but they couldn't tell if they were the missing ones. Then Bob pointed to the ranch house.

"Look. There's the truck. I wonder what Red is up to."

"Let's see how our steers are doing," said Ted. "Then we can ride back to the house and see."

When the boys got back, the steers were gone. The ropes went from the trees down to the little brook. The ropes and brook seemed to go right into a rock wall.

CHAPTER X

The boys followed the ropes into some bushes that grew
around the little brook. "Look," said Ted, "there are some
branches broken off one of the bushes." Bob pushed one of the
bushes aside and saw a hole where the brook ran through
the wall.

"Here's where they went!" yelled Ted. "There must be an opening on the other side of the wall."

"But this hole isn't high enough for a steer to walk through," said Bob. "It's wide enough, but the steers would have to crawl."

"Look at the brook, Bob!" Ted was shouting with excitement. "It's very deep right at the hole. The steers could walk in the water and get through the hole. Our horses could do it, too."

52

Ted stood in the water and looked through the hole. "I can see light on the other side. Let's go through."

Bob followed Ted into the water and through the hole. It was hard to keep their heads above water but the boys got through. Bob and Ted stopped as they came through the opening on the other side of the walls. They found themselves in a big field with grass and trees.

"Gosh," said Bob. "These hills aren't like the ones over in the center of the ranch. These aren't all rock!"

"Look, said Ted, "there must be two hundred steers in here."

The boys looked all around. The walls were white. They didn't look like rock at all.

"The walls are covered with salt. That must be salt, Bob! That's why the steers came in here."

"Gosh!" Bob couldn't say anything else.

"I wonder where our horses are," said Ted. At that moment, at the far end of the field, a brown horse ran from behind a tree. A black-and-white one was with him.

"They're here!" cried Bob. "They're here!"

"Let's hurry back and tell Uncle Will. We'd better hurry. He may let the men talk him into taking Millar's herd."

The boys led their horses through the hole in the wall. When they were outside, they climbed into the saddles and rode as fast as they could to the house. Buzz was waiting for them when they got there.

"We found them, Buzz, we found the missing steers!" Ted shouted.

"You found them! Oh my gosh! Where? Why didn't you get back fifteen minutes ago? Red went back into town. When he came back, he told the men that Millar didn't buy the cattle there. Lefty talked him into going out there after the herd."

"Come on, Ted, let's ride out and stop them!"

"You won't be able to catch them," said Buzz. "They must be there by now."

"I'll stop them." Ted ran to the ranch bell and began to ring it as fast and hard as he could.

"Will they hear him?" asked Bob.

"They'll hear him all the way into town."

Ted started for the house to tell Uncle Will the news, but just then Will came to one of the windows of the house.

"What's going on?" he asked. "That bell is only for trouble."

"Uncle Will," shouted Bob, "we found the cattle! We found them!"

"Hey, what are you doing out of bed?" Buzz ran for the house.

"Never mind about the bed. Tell me about the cattle. That will cure my broken leg. Ring that bell again and get those boys back here. Are you sure about the cattle?" Uncle Will was so excited, the words all came out at once.

Bob rang the ranch bell again while Ted told Uncle Will the whole story.

"Well!" Uncle Will shook his head. "You boys really learned to be cowboys fast. You're pretty smart fellows. Here I thought I knew all about this ranch and you found a spot I didn't even know was there!"

"We had help," said Ted. "There were two pretty smart horses helping us."

Soon the cowboys came galloping up to the house.

"What's up?" asked Red. "We were just about to take the steers away from Millar when we heard the bell."

"We caught you just in time," said Will.

As soon as the cowboys heard the story, they headed for

56

the brook. When they got to the little hole in the rock wall, Red splashed through it with the boys.

"We should make use of this good grass! I'll get some of the men to make the hole bigger. Then the cattle can get through it any time."

Lefty came through the hole. He counted the steers that were in the little field. "They're all here! All of the steers that were missing."

Lefty looked very sad. "We almost hurt that poor fellow Millar, and he didn't do anything but brand his own cattle."

"Well, the boys stopped us in time," said Red. "Good thing you came out for a visit, fellows. Now, let's get busy. I want that hole big enough to ride a horse through."

Lefty went out to get some men to help him. Soon the hole was big enough to drive a wagon through. Then they all rode back to the ranch house.

Everyone was hungry. They carried Uncle Will downstairs and Buzz cooked a fine dinner. He brought out a cake that made Bob's and Ted's mouths water. The boys finished the first piece and asked for another.

"Now you're eating like cowboys." Red smiled.

When they were finished, Uncle Will said, "I think we'll have to do something for the boys. They were the ones who found the lost steers. What would you like, boys?"

Bob said, "Ted was the one who found them. He should get what he would like to have."

"Well, Ted, what do you want?"

Ted thought for a while. "I think I'd like to take something out to Mr. Millar. We almost made a lot of trouble for him. He had a right to be angry at us for coming around all the time. What do you think, Buzz? What about a cake?"

"Sure," said Buzz. "That's easy."

"One more thing," said Uncle Will. "We're getting too many horses in the corral. Do you boys think that you can help me find homes for Dusty and Storm?"

The boys didn't know what to say. "Well, speak up," said Uncle Will. "If you don't want them, I'll find someone else."

"We'll take them, Uncle Will," said both boys. "Boy, will we ever take them!"

The next morning the boys rode out to take the cake to Mr. Millar.

They explained all that had happened. Mr. Millar rested while they talked. When they said they were sorry for watching him so closely, he said to forget it.

"Just one thing—where *did* you get the cattle?" asked Bob.

Millar took a paper out of his shirt.

"I bought them from a fellow down the river. Brought them in at night."

"Why at night?"

"Too much work to do when the sun is up," said Millar with a smile. "Come on, boys, you're just in time to help me cut these logs."

58

OTHER BOOKS INCLUDED IN THE
INTERESTING READING PROGRAM

Adventure in Space

Buried Gold

First Adventure at Sea

First Men in Space

Great Moments in American History

Indian Fighters, The

Mary Elizabeth and Mr. Lincoln

Teddy Roosevelt

Ten Great Moments in Sports

Your Guide to the FOLLETT Interesting Reading Series